Fresh
Pickings

Carol Barrow

Text copyright © Carol Barrow and Gatehouse Books Ltd 2004
Illustrations, Heather Dickinson
Cover Design, Gatehouse Books Ltd
Photograph, Anne Chester
Editor, Steph Prior
Published and distributed by Gatehouse Books Ltd.
Hulme Adult Education Centre, Stretford Road, Manchester M15 5FQ
Printed by RAP Ltd., Oldham.
ISBN 1 84231 011 9
British Library cataloguing in publication data:
A catalogue record for this book is available from the British Library

This writing was originated and developed in the course of the Gatehouse
"New Readers New Writers Roadshow" project, with funding from the Royal Mail
Group's Stepping Stone Fund.

Gatehouse is grateful for continued financial support from Manchester City Council,
and for financial assistance from the Royal Mail Group's Stepping Stone Fund for the
development of this publication.

Our thanks for their ongoing support to Manchester Adult Education Service.

Thanks to the New Readers New Writers Roadshow Reading Circle: Z. & Y.Affridi,
J.Barker, D.Blake, K.Claffey, B.Farrell, S.Fitzpatrick, J.S.Forrest, L.Green,
J.Garvey, C.Hokat, B.Lake, B.Lucy, P.Martin, C.Morrison, S.Naznin, D. Quinton,
A.Roscoe, S.Ryan, A.Simpson, M.Taylor, M.Tetteh-Lartey, M.Toohill, F.Wallwork,
H.Williams, M.Wells.

Gatehouse is a member of The Federation of Worker Writers & Community
Publishers.
Gatehouse is a charity registered in England no. 1011042.

Gatehouse provides an opportunity for writers to express their thoughts and
feelings on aspects of their lives.

The views expressed are not necessarily those of Gatehouse.

When I was young,
we had a gooseberry bush
in the garden.

We used to pick
the gooseberries
so my mam
could make a pie.

The gooseberries
were hard and hairy
and tasted bitter,
but the pie,
when cooked,
was sweet.

7

Our neighbour
had red rhubarb
in her garden.
Some times
my mam and the neighbour
used to swap
and we would have rhubarb pie.

I liked the colour
of the rhubarb.
It was very red and crisp
and when we picked it,
it snapped.

Also I remember
when we used to go
to the potato shop.
The man gave us
peas in the pod
to eat.

PEAS

MELONS
PEACHES
half
price

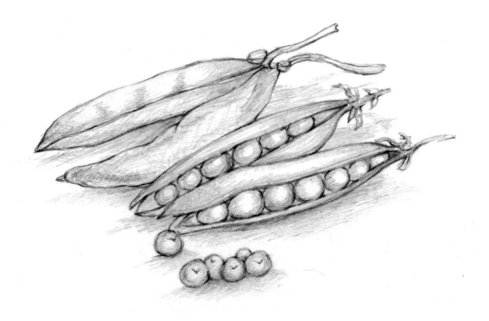

The pods were very green.

They squeaked

and popped

when we opened them.

The peas were hard
but sweet
at the same time.
That was the best thing
about going to the potato shop.

About the Author

When I was fifty-one
I went to an English class
because I thought I was a bad speller.
I couldn't understand
why I could read a word
but not be able to write it down.
The tutor, Chris Hayes,
realised I had a problem.
Now I've found out that I am dyslexic.
Now I am going on a special course
to help me find ways
of coping with my Dyslexia.

I won't let this problem stop me.
I do an Art class, computers and English.
This year I took part in a short writing workshop
Gatehouse had put on
as part of their
New Readers New Writers Roadshow.
I wrote this story there.
I didn't think it was any good
but it meant something to me.
I couldn't believe it
when Gatehouse told me
they wanted to publish it as a book!
I hope to continue
with my classes and my writing.
I'm not going to give up on myself.

Carol Barrow

Gatehouse Books

Gatehouse is a unique publisher

Our writers are adults who are developing their basic
reading and writing skills. Their ideas and experiences
make fascinating material for any reader, but are
particularly relevant for adults working on their reading
and writing skills. The writing strikes a chord - a shared
experience of struggling against many odds.

The format of our books is clear and uncluttered. The
language is familiar and the text is often line-broken, so
that each line ends at a natural pause.

Gatehouse books are both popular and respected within
Adult Basic Education throughout the English speaking
world. They are also a valuable resource within
secondary schools, Social Services and within the Prison
Education Service and Probation Services.

Booklist available

Gatehouse Books
Hulme Adult Education Centre
Stretford Road
Manchester
M15 5FQ
Tel/Fax: 0161 226 7152
E-mail: office@gatehousebooks.org.uk
Website: www.gatehousebooks.org.uk